THIS LITTLE TIGER BOOK BELONGS TO:

_____

_____

_____

_____

LITTLE TIGER PRESS
An imprint of Magi Publications
1 The Coda Centre, 189 Munster Road, London SW6 6AW
This paperback edition published 2000
First published in Great Britain 2000
Text © 2000 Michael Coleman
Illustrations © 2000 Tim Warnes
Michael Coleman and Tim Warnes have asserted
their rights to be identified as the author and illustrator
of this work under the Copyright, Designs and
Patents Act, 1988.
Printed in Belgium by Proost NV, Turnhout
All rights reserved • ISBN 1 85430 643 X
3 5 7 9 10 8 6 4 2

Michael Coleman
Tim Warnes

George
&
Sylvia

A Tale of True Love

LITTLE TIGER PRESS
London

George was madly
in love with Sylvia.
And Sylvia was madly
in love with George.

The trouble was
that neither of them could
pluck up the courage to tell
each other how they felt.

George thought that
Sylvia couldn't possibly
love him because
he was too big and fat.
"Sylvia's slim,
Sylvia's trim,
but I've got a shape
that's really grim!"
he sighed to himself.

As for Sylvia,
she thought George
couldn't possibly love
her because she was
small and skinny.
"George is big,
George is strong,
but I've got a shape
that's gone all wrong,"
she grumbled.

So George decided there
was only one thing to do.
He would have to
change his shape.
"I'm going to be slim,
and I'm going to be trim,
and then *my* shape
won't be so grim!"
he said.

Sylvia had decided
to do something, too.
She was going to
change her shape as well.
"I'm going to be big,
and I'm going to be strong,
and then *my* shape
won't be all wrong,"
she said to herself.

So every day, George tried to make himself slimmer . . .

George tried to make himself trimmer . . .

and Sylvia tried to make herself stronger.

But nothing really worked.
George's shape hardly changed.
"I'm still not slim, I'm still not trim.
I've still got a shape that's really grim,"
he groaned.

Sylvia's shape didn't change either.
"I'm still not big, I'm still not strong.
I've still got a shape that's gone all wrong!"
she moaned.

George decided to think of some
other way to change his shape.
He wound tight-fitting vines
around himself, squeezing . . .

and squeezing until he
could hardly breathe.

While Sylvia tied
pillows and pads
in place . . .

VALENTINE'S
fancy dress
PARTY!

TONIGHT!

until she could
hardly move.

It was the evening of the Valentine's
Fancy Dress Party and George felt
he was ready to meet his love at last.
"Now I look slim, now I look trim –
even if I'm not!"
he said happily.

And Sylvia looked at herself
in her mirror and cried,
"Now I look big, now I look strong –
even if I'm not!"

When Sylvia and George arrived at the Party, they didn't recognise each other.
"Are you looking for someone?" asked Sylvia.
George scowled at Sylvia.
"Yes, I am," he said.

"Someone wonderful.
Someone slim, someone trim,
not someone with a shape
that's really grim."

"Well," said Sylvia grandly.
"I'm waiting for someone special, too.
Someone big, someone strong!
Not someone with a shape
that's gone all wrong!"

"The only thing is," said George with a sigh, "I can't see Sylvia anywhere."
"And I can't see George anywhere, either," said Sylvia miserably.

Sadly, they both turned
to leave . . .

until suddenly George
realised what Sylvia had said.
"You're looking for George?
Not big, fat George?"
"George isn't big and fat," cried
Sylvia. "He's tall and strong."

Tall and strong was he?
George puffed out his chest
with pride.
Pee-oooonngggg!
went the vines all around him.
"Then you're looking for me!"
he shouted.
  "I'm tall, I'm strong!
  This is *my* shape and
  it's not all wrong!"

Then Sylvia remembered what George had said.
"You're looking for Sylvia? Not short, skinny Sylvia?"
"Sylvia's not short and skinny!" shouted George.
"She's slim! She's trim!"

Sylvia pulled out all her padding, and threw it away.
"Then you're looking for me!" she cried happily.
"I'm slim! I'm trim!
This is *my* shape and
it's not really grim!"

And so it was that George and Sylvia found each other, and lived happily ever after.

"I'm big, I'm strong, she'll love me long," said George.

"I'm slim, I'm trim,
just right for him!"
said Sylvia.

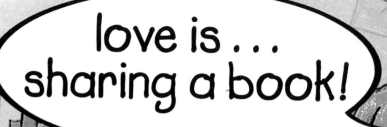

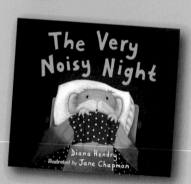
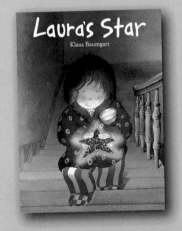
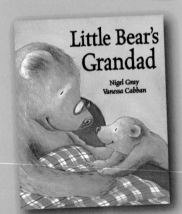

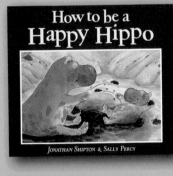
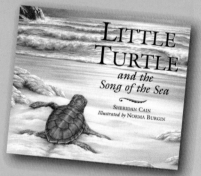